PINOCCHIO

Chris McEwan

⚓

DOUBLEDAY
NEW YORK TORONTO LONDON SYDNEY AUCKLAND

This book belongs to . . .

_____

_____

_____

PUBLISHED BY DOUBLEDAY
a division of Bantam Doubleday Dell Publishing Group, Inc.
666 Fifth Avenue, New York, New York 10103

DOUBLEDAY
and the portrayal of an anchor with a dolphin
are trademarks of Doubleday, a division of
Bantam Doubleday Dell Publishing Group, Inc.

First published in England by William Collins Sons & Co. Ltd.

Library of Congress Cataloging-in-Publication Data
McEwan, Chris.
Pinocchio/Chris McEwan.—1st ed. in the U.S.A.
p.   cm.
Adaptation of: Avventure di Pinocchio/Carlo Collodi.
"First published in England by William Collins"—T.p. verso.
Summary: A wooden puppet full of tricks and mischief, with a
talent for getting into and out of trouble, wants more than anything
else to become a real boy.
[1. Fairy tales.   2. Puppets—Fiction.]   I. Collodi, Carlo,
1826–1890.   Avventure di Pinocchio.   II. Title.
PZ8.M4578Pi   1990
[E]—dc20   89-23733   CIP   AC
ISBN 0-385-41327-0
ISBN 0-385-41328-9 (lib. bdg.)

Text and illustrations copyright © 1989 by Chris McEwan

Once upon a time there was a piece of wood.

It stood in the corner of a carpenter's shop. One day the carpenter decided that he would use the wood to make a leg for his table. But when he picked up his axe to begin work, to his very great surprise he heard a tiny voice saying ,"Please don't strike me *too* hard!" And every time the carpenter touched the wood with a saw or a plane or a chisel, he heard, to his even greater astonishment the same tiny voice calling, "Oh! You hurt me!" or "Stop! You're tickling me!" Just then a jolly little man entered the carpenter's shop. His name was Geppetto and he was looking for some wood to make a puppet. The carpenter was delighted to get rid of the strange piece of wood, so he gave it to Geppetto.

As soon as he arrived home, Geppetto began work. "I shall make a fine puppet," he said; "he will be like a son to me and I shall send him to school just like a real boy."

But as the puppet took shape, strange things began to happen. The eyes began to move and stare at him, the mouth to laugh and poke fun at him, and as for the nose…it had a life of its own.

"What name shall I give this naughty puppet?" said Geppetto to himself. "I know, I shall call him Pinocchio!"

The puppet was no sooner finished than it ran away! And just as
Geppetto caught him, the policemen shouted, "STOP!"

While poor Geppetto tried to explain the commotion to the policemen, Pinocchio escaped again and ran home! But as he reached the safety of Geppetto's house, he heard someone calling his name. A large cricket creeping up the wall said, "I have a great truth to tell you, Pinocchio. Woe to those boys who do not obey their parents and who run away from home! They will never do any good in this world and sooner or later they will be sorry."

But Pinocchio said, "If I stay here I shall be sent to school! I want only to amuse myself and be a vagabond from morning to night!" And he leapt around the room, throwing things in the air.

"Don't you know that if you don't go to school you will grow up to be a great donkey?" said the cricket. "Poor Pinocchio, I am sorry for you, because you are only a puppet, and what is worse, you have a wooden head."

At that, Pinocchio threw a wooden rooster's head at the cricket and cried, "Here's a wooden head for you!" Then more quietly he sighed, "I don't want to be a wooden puppet! I wish I could be a *real* boy!"

"Ah," said the cricket, "to make that wish come true you will have to learn to do as you are told."

So Pinocchio promised to go to school. Kind old Geppetto made him
a suit and bought him a special schoolbook.

But the next day, on his way to school, Pinocchio saw a puppet theater, and sold his schoolbook to buy a ticket!

Harlequin and Punchinello were on the stage, and when they saw Pinocchio they called out to him to come and join them.

Then all the puppets in the company shouted, "Here's Pinocchio!
Here's our brother Pinocchio! Hurrah for Pinocchio!"
But suddenly silence fell. The Showman had appeared!

All the poor puppets trembled with fear as the Showman roared, "Harlequin! Punchinello! Where is that Pinocchio who has ruined my show? Bring him to me! He is made of nice dry wood and I'm sure he will make a good fire to roast my dinner. Pinocchio wriggled and shouted and cried until at last the Showman said, "Very well, you shall be spared. But now I haven't enough wood for my fire." And he ordered them to bring Harlequin instead!

Pinocchio wept and begged the Showman to pardon poor Harlequin, but to no avail. "In that case I know my duty," cried Pinocchio; "bind me and throw *me* into the fire. It is not right that my truest friend should die for me!" At this, all the puppets began to weep until finally the Showman himself opened his arms to Pinocchio, saying, "You are a good brave boy!" When the puppets knew that their brothers were safe, they jumped and danced and sang for joy.

When Pinocchio finally set off for home, the Showman called after him and gave him a gift of six gold pieces, a reward for a true heart.

Pinocchio marched along happily, jingling the coins in his pocket.
But on his way he met two rascals, who invited him to dinner.
Pinocchio eagerly accepted their invitation. When the bill for dinner
arrived, however, his new friends had disappeared.

When Pinocchio left the inn, the streets were empty and silent. Inside his head he heard a voice telling him to go home at once, but it was too late! Out of the darkness he was set upon by criminals, who bound him and gagged him and ran off into the night.

Tears rolled down the cheeks of the unhappy puppet, until a kind
fairy, hearing his cries, flew down and took pity on him. She took
him to her home and called the doctors.

But naughty Pinocchio wouldn't take his medicine, so the awful
black rabbits came to take him away.

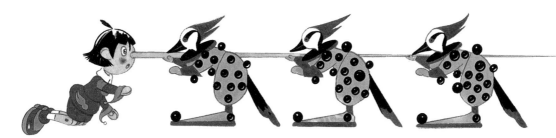

Pinocchio was so frightened that he drank the medicine down in one gulp, and the rabbits left, grumbling between their teeth. Then the good fairy asked Pinocchio why the criminals had attacked him and he explained that they wanted to steal his gold pieces.

"Where are the gold pieces now?" asked the fairy.

"I've lost them," answered Pinocchio, which was a lie, for he had them safely hidden in his pocket. No sooner had he told this lie than his nose grew two inches longer!

"Where did you lose them?" the fairy asked.

"In the wood nearby," replied the naughty puppet. At this second lie, his nose grew longer still.

The fairy said, "If you lost them nearby, we can search for them."

Pinocchio was confused, "Oh now I remember," he said. "I didn't lose them, I swallowed them when I was drinking your medicine." At this third lie, his nose grew so long that poor Pinocchio could not move in any direction without hitting the bed or the walls or the door!

The fairy laughed and laughed. "Lies, my dear Pinocchio," she said, "are easy to recognize. There are two sorts, those with short legs and those with long noses. Your sort have long noses."

Pinocchio was very ashamed. He tried to run away but couldn't because his nose wouldn't fit through the door, so he cried and screamed until at last the fairy took pity on him. She clapped her hands and a flock of woodpeckers flew in and pecked away the ridiculous nose until it was its usual size once more. Then the fairy said to him, "Remember, little Pinocchio, that only when you have learned to be good and kind will you be truly happy."

As he left, Pinocchio promised the fairy that he would be a good boy, do as he was told, and go to school. But on the way home he met the two rascals again. As they walked along together, the fox told Pinocchio about the Field of Miracles, where, if you buried your gold, a wonderful tree would grow laden with hundreds and hundreds of gold pieces. Pinocchio grew very excited, "Oh, what a very fine gentleman I shall be!" he cried. And forgetting his promise to the fairy, he set off at once to bury his gold pieces. The next day he hurried back to the magic field, but he could see no tree covered in gold. So he dug down deep, but there were no gold pieces either! Pinocchio was puzzled. But then he heard a noise, and looking round, he saw a large parrot sitting nearby. The parrot told him how the fox and the cat had crept back under cover of darkness and stolen the gold.

Pinocchio grew extremely cross. "Never mind," said the parrot.
"Climb on my back and I will take you to the fairy's house."

When Pinocchio, sadder and a tiny bit wiser, arrived at the fairy's house, he felt very uncomfortable. Perhaps the kind fairy wouldn't forgive him. After all, he had broken his promise to her.

He plucked up his courage and knocked at the door. A snail looked down from the upstairs window. "Hurry, dear snail," called Pinocchio, "for I am tired and cold and hungry." But snails are never in a hurry and the little puppet had a long time to learn patience while he waited for the door to be opened.

While Pinocchio drank the tea that the snail had brought for him, the fairy watched with a stern expression on her face. When he had finished she said, "Oh, Pinocchio, when will you learn that bad things happen to bad boys? I forgive you this time and because I want you to be happy, I will make a bargain with you. If you promise to be a good and obedient boy for one whole month, then I will grant your dearest wish. Tell me what you wish, Pinocchio."

The little puppet jumped up and down with excitement. "I wish, oh, how I wish I could be a *real* boy!"

So for one whole month, right up until the last day, Pinocchio kept his word and studied hard and was very, very good…

And so on the last day of the month, the fairy planned a grand party, and Pinocchio went to invite his school friend to the feast.

But instead of returning to the fairy's house, the two friends went off
to Playland, where there was no school, only amusements and games!

The problem with Playland, however, was that eventually all the children turned into donkeys, just as the cricket had warned.

At first when Pinocchio became a donkey, he worked in a circus, and it was very hard work indeed. The ringmaster was cruel and used the whip to teach him tricks. The only food he was given was dry hay. Oh, how bitterly did Pinocchio regret his naughtiness, and with what sadness did he remember the wise words of the cricket and the good fairy.

Then one day he stumbled and went lame. The cruel ringmaster, having no more use for him, threw the little donkey into the sea. But no sooner did he hit the water than the donkey turned back into Pinocchio.

Pinocchio swam as fast as he could, not caring where he was going, when suddenly he saw the most terrible sight of his life. Rushing toward him, with its enormous mouth open wide and showing rows of dreadful teeth, was a gigantic shark. Poor Pinocchio tried to escape, but the monster was too powerful for him. Closer and closer it came until with a SNAP! of its mighty jaws it swallowed the little puppet whole! With a great rush and tumble of water Pinocchio was swept deep down inside the shark until at last he came to rest in what looked like a huge dark cavern.

Taking his courage in both hands, Pinocchio made his way through
the gloom deep inside the shark's body. Far off he could see a tiny
light. As he got nearer he could see it was a candle standing on a table.
And by the table was a chair, and sitting on the chair was none other
than old Geppetto! He had been swallowed by the shark while
searching for Pinocchio and had thought never to see his wooden boy
again.
They greeted each other joyfully, and while the great shark slept, they
tiptoed through the awful teeth and out of its mouth to freedom.

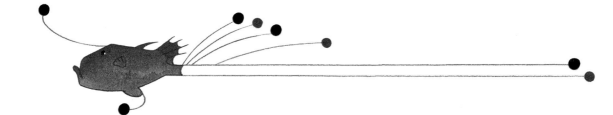

At that moment the dreadful beast awoke! Pulling Geppetto with him, Pinocchio swam and swam until he had no strength left.

Just in time some friendly fish came to their rescue. Together they flew across the waves until they reached the shore and safety.

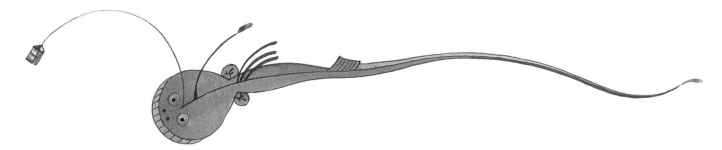

After they had rested, Pinocchio and Geppetto set off on the long road home. Pinocchio was so happy to have found Geppetto again, and so glad not to be a donkey, or inside a shark, that from that day onward he worked hard and earned enough to pay for all their needs. When evening came he practiced his reading and writing. He was good and obedient without even trying!

One night after he had been working even harder than usual, Pinocchio finally climbed into bed at midnight. As he slept he dreamed of the fairy. She smiled down at him and gave him a kiss and said, "Brave Pinocchio! You have a good heart and have done well. I forgive you for being so naughty. Be good in the future and you will be happy."

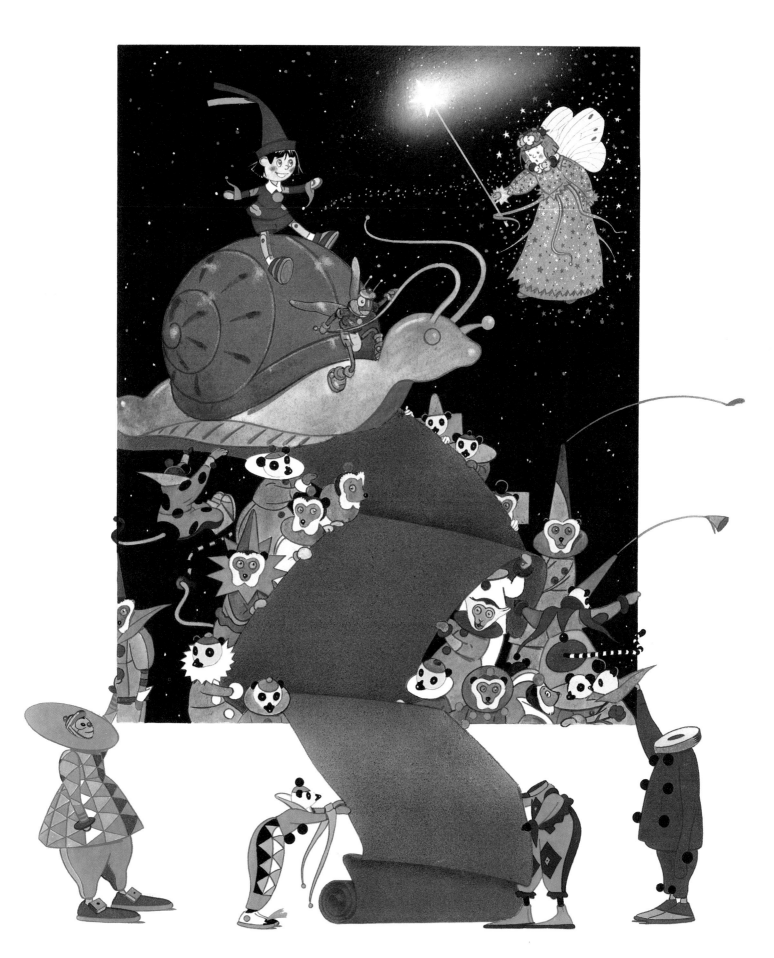

And when Pinocchio awoke the next morning, his dearest wish had come true. He was no longer a puppet but a real boy!